For William and Isabel

PEACHTREE PUBLISHERS
1700 Chattahoochee Avenue
Atlanta, Georgia 30318-2112
www.peachtree-online.com

Text and Illustration © 2007 by John Butler
First published by Orchard Books in Great Britain, 2007

10 9 8 7 6 5 4 3 2 1
Printed in Singapore

Artwork created in acrylic and colored pencil

Library of Congress Cataloging-in-Publication Data

Butler, John, 1952-
Can you growl like a bear? / written and illustrated by
John Butler. -- 1st ed.
p. cm.
Summary: In rhyming text, the reader is asked to mimic a variety
of animal noises in preparation for a good night's sleep.
ISBN 13: 978-1-56145-396-2
ISBN 10: 1-56145-396-X
[1. Animal sounds--Fiction. 2. Animals--Fiction. 3. Bedtime--Fiction.
4. Stories in rhyme.] I. Title.
PZ8.3.B9788Cag 2007
[E]--dc22
2006103192

www.johnbutlerart.com

Can You Growl Like a Bear?

John Butler

PEACHTREE
ATLANTA

Listen to the animals.
What noises do you hear?

Come along and join the fun!

Speak up loud and clear.

Can you **growl** like a bear,

rolling in the snow?

Can you chatter
like a chimp,
swinging to and fro?

Can you **click** like a dolphin,
swimming through the seas?

Can you **buzz** like a honeybee, floating on a breeze?

Can you trumpet

Everyone is quiet now.
You can't hear a peep.

Can you **Snuffle** like a panda, snuggling up for the night?

Can you **howl**
like a wolf,
keeping watch late
at night?

Can you **squawk** like a cockatoo, soaring in the sky?

It's time to gently close your eyes

and fall fast asleep.